What's Michael?

Planet of the Cats

Story and Art:
Makoto Kobayashi

Translation:
Dana Lewis & Lea Hernandez

Dark Horse Manga™

Lettering and Retouch:
Sno Cone Studios

publisher
Mike Richardson

series editor
Philip Simon

series executive editor
Toren Smith for **Studio Proteus**

collection editor
Chris Warner

designers
Mark Cox and **Tina Alessi**

art director
Lia Ribacchi

English-language version produced by
Dark Horse Manga.

What's Michael? Vol. 11: Planet of the Cats

This volume collects What's Michael? stories
from issues forty-nine through fifty and fifty-two
through fifty-nine of the Dark Horse comic-book
series **Super Manga Blast!**

The artwork of this volume has been produced as
a mirror-image of the original Japanese edition to
conform to English-language standards.

Dark Horse Manga
A division of Dark Horse Comics, Inc.
10956 SE Main Street
Milwaukie, OR 97222

darkhorse.com

To find a comics shop in your area, call the
Comic Shop Locator Service toll-free at
1-888-266-4226

First edition: April 2006
ISBN 10: 1-59307-525-1
ISBN 13: 978-1-59307-525-5
10 9 8 7 6 5 4 3 2 1
Printed in Canada

DO YOU KNOW THIS CAT?

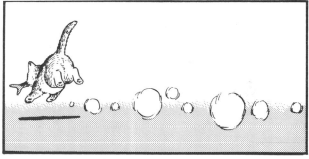

DOES THAT CAT COME AROUND HERE OFTEN?

HUH?!

ALL TH' DAG-BLASTED TIME!

HE'S TH' *BIG BOSSMAN* 'ROUND HERE.

HOW CAN THAT BE?

HE STOPS BY MY HOUSE ALMOST EVERY *DAY*...

...AND I LIVE *TWO MILES* AWAY!

HAHH? THAT STICKY-PAWED CAT COMES *ALL THET WAY T' ROB ME?*

I KNOW THAT KITTY, TOO!

HE SLEEPS IN OUR *GARDEN* ALL THE TIME!

HE MUST REALLY *LOVE* IT--

--OUR HOME'S OVER *THREE MILES* AWAY!

...!

SAYURI SUZUKI, BAR HOSTESS, B WARD...

YEAH, I'VE SEEN THE CAT BEFORE.

HE USES THE *CROSSWALK* IN FRONT OF OUR CLUB.

4

SEIICHI ASANO, FARMER, A WARD...

CHARLES? CAT? OH, *HIM.*

HE WAS EYEIN' OUR *CHICKENS,* SO I *CLOCKED* HIM GOOD WITH A *ROCK!*

THE MAGNIFICENT YAMAMOTO, ANIMAL PSYCHIC, C WARD...

I SEE ZEE *CHAT* UNDER A *BREEDGE.*

IT LOOKS AZ EEF HE HEV *LE TUMMY ACHE,* SO I ASSK TO HEEM, "ARE YOU *LE OKAY?"* "OUI, I AM *LE OKAY,"* HE TELLS ME.

SHHAAAAA

HM ...?

CHARLES!

5

IT'S RAINING *BUCKETS*, AND YOU STILL CAME TO SEE ME...?

POOR THING. HERE, SOME DRIED SARDINES.

YOW!!

CHOMPF! CHOMPF!

HEH HEH.

TAKE YOUR TIME!

I FOUND OUT YOU'VE GOT A *HUGE TURF*, CHARLES.

I HAD NO *IDEA!*

BUT... YOU MAKE TIME FOR *ME.*

WHY DON'T YOU *LIVE* HERE? YOU CAN COME AND GO AS YOU PLEASE.

CHOMPF MNCH

SHLRRP

PRROWW...

6

CHARLES! IT'S *POURING!*

AT LEAST STAY UNTIL THE RAIN STOPS!

....
....

HE MUST HAVE AN *INCREDIBLE* OWNER...

SHAAAAA

YAW?!

7

8

THE END

MINI-MIKE IN LOVE

IT WAS A BEAUTIFUL DAY, AND *MINI-MIKE*, HIS HEART BURSTING WITH JOY, RUSHED OUTSIDE TO PLAY!

GOSH, IT'S GOOD TO BE ALIVE!

PRROWR!

OOF!

OOF!

MRT! NRRT!

RRT?

TEE HEE HEE HEE!

WOOKIT THAT WIDDLE TUMMY!

WHAT A *CUTIE!*

MNNT...

POOR LITTLE *SUE*. SHE *NEVER* GETS TO GO OUTSIDE.

SHE MUST BE *DYING* TO, HUH?

HOW 'BOUT WE GET A PLACE WITH A *GARDEN*? Y'KNOW, FOR *SUE*...?

HONEY! *REALLY?!*

TMP

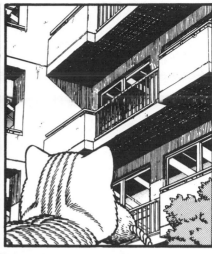

TMP
TMP

WASTIN' YER *TIME*, YEP.

THAT CUTIE ON THE *FIFTH FLOOR* MOVED OUT *YESTER-DAY*.

EH ...?

NUH... NUH...

THE END

THE RETURN OF DRACULA!

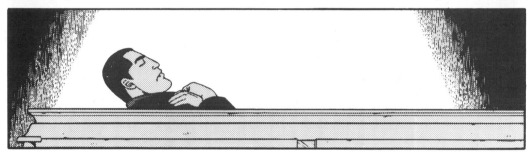

DRACULA! THE WORLD'S MOST FEARSOME VAMPIRE!

UNDEAD FOR NEARLY A MILLENNIUM!

YET...

...WITHOUT HUMAN BLOOD FOR A CENTURY!

THE CASE FOR VAMPIRISM
IDIOT'S GUIDE TO VAMPIRES
HEALTHY VAMPIRE
VAMP AND PROUD!
SMART BLOOD-SUCKING
SUNNYDALE FIELD GUIDE
THINK BEFORE YOU SUCK!
GOOD BLOOD, BAD BLOOD
PRACTICAL VAMPIRISM
OUR FANGS, OUR SELVES
TAXES FOR THE WORKING VAMPIRE

RACTICAL VAMPIRIS

BLOOD, BLOOD, BLOOD
BLOODSUCKING BASICS

PRACTICAL VAMPIRISM
PRACTICAL VAMPIRISM

PRACTICAL VAMPIRE TIP #1:

THE EASIEST GIRL TO CATCH AND DRAIN IS THE ONE STANDING STILL!

EASY ENOUGH ...!

PRACTICAL TIP #2:

PHOTOGRAPHERS CAN GET A GIRL TO DO *ANYTHING!*

PARDON ME, MISS!

I'M FROM *MODERN WEEKLY'S* "SHOW US YOUR PANTIES" SPECIAL! HOW ABOUT A SHOT?

OOOH ...!

OH, PLEASE? JUST ONE?!

I'M SORRY TO BEG, BUT IT'S MY *JOB!*

WHO, *ME?!*

NO *WAY! I* COULDN'T POSSIBLY--

REALLY *FAST*, OKAY?

TAKE IT QUICK!

READY!

ONE, TWO...

THREE!

FWPP!

KSHAK!

YAAAHHH!

THANK... YOU...

PRACTICAL TIP #3:

A VAMPIRE WHO **NEEDS** BLOOD CAN'T BE TOO **PICKY**, CAN HE?

BLOOD IS BLOOD, AFTER ALL.

HRM.

SHE LOOKS **TOUGH** ...

...BUT SHE'LL HAVE TO DO.

HEYYY THERE, LI'L CUTIE!

HOW ABOUT DINNER **AND** BREAKFAST?

....
....

19

THE END

TALKING WITH THE ANIMALS

21

RAWWN! ROWWN!

THAT'S ENOUGH, MIKE!

THIS IS MY SISTER! BE NICE!

I SHOULD HAVE EXPECTED THIS!

LEAVE IT TO MY BIG SIS TO KNOW "KITTY."

OHH ...!

POPO!

....

MYA! MRRAW!

MYA!

THANK YOU!

HELLO TO YOU, TOO!

ER...ACTUALLY
SHE SAID, "YOU'RE
IN MY *SPOT!*
MOVE IT!"

MRRT
MRRRT!

MRRN!
MRT!

...?

OKAY, THEN,
WHAT'S *HE*
SAYING?

"LOOK,
A *PEN.*"

AWWN!
AHM!

SQUEE!

23

SHE'S SAYING, "DO IT WITH ME!"

SHAYYYY!

SPAHHH!

R–REALLY?

HM?

KRIT!

HOWDY, HANA! GOOD TO SEE YOU!

OH, HEE HEE, HI!

IS SIS TREATING YOU RIGHT?

AAAH... HEY...

WHAT...?

25

NARA-ZUKE... PICKLES?

VACUUM CLEANER!

OH...

ALL RIGHT.

WOW...

OH, HE SAID, "I WANT A NEW CAR," AND I SAID, "ARE YOU *NUTS?*"

SIS, *TELL ME!* WHAT'D YOU *SAY?*

HM?

ROUUN! MAWWN!

YOUR LITTER BOX NEEDS SCOOPING?

JUST A MINUTE!

THE GOOD WIFE SPEAKS KITTY, BABY, AND HUSBAND.

THE END

WALKING WITH THE ANIMALS

28

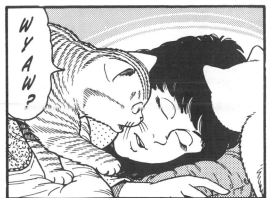

YOU CLOSE YOUR EYES!

HM...

LIKE THIS?

... ...

READY!

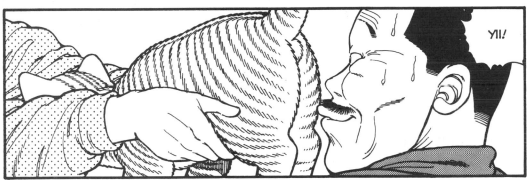

YII!

PKK KRAK

HEH.

37

SOME COUPLES ENJOY *SIMPLE PLEASURES* (WEIRD, BUT SIMPLE).

THE END

ONLY FORTY MINUTES BY BUS FROM DYNAMIC UENOHARA, IN LOVELY YAMANASHI PREFECTURE!

TOKYO KONBAYASHI LAND!

ACROSS A RUSTIC SUSPENSION BRIDGE, FAMOUS FOR SUICIDES...

DON'T DO IT! THINK AGAIN!

...INTO A LAND OF DREAMS!

POK POK

FWEEE

TOKYO KONBAYASHI LAND!

KONBAYASHI RESTAURANT
SERVES A MOUTH WATERING
ARRAY OF DELICACIES!

VISIT THE KONBAYASHI
STORE! BUY ONE OF EVERYTHING!

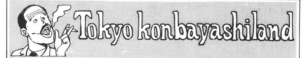

Tokyo konbayashiland

RIDE THE
PEACE TRAIN
IN MAKKOI
WORLD!

THE
MERRY-GO-ROUND OF
LOVE!

TOKYO KONBAYASHI LAND: BANKRUPT... AND EIGHT HUNDRED MILLION DOLLARS IN DEBT.

ACCORDING TO RUMOR, CHAIRMAN KONBAYASHI WAS LAST SEEN STANDING ON SUICIDE BRIDGE...

DON'T DO IT! THINK AGAIN!

THE END

THE INVITATION

47

KCHAK!

PLEASE *FORGIVE ME?*

WHAT WERE WE TALKING ABOUT?

RIGHT.

SO SUN- DAY--

MICHAEL! NO! DON'T!

TMP TMP TMP TMP TMP

....
....

....
....

TMP TMP TMP TMP TMP

....
....

KCHAK!

HA HA HA! I SHOULDN'T *LAUGH!*

BUT *MICHAEL!* HEEE! HE FELL OFF THE *TV!* BUT HE'S *FINE.*

IS HE?

WHERE WERE WE?

UMM ...

NORIO ISHIKAWA: BECOMING A **DOG PERSON.**

50

THE END

MICHAEL, AH *HATE YOU!*

TEARFUL ALYCE

FINE! WHO CARES?

BE THAT WAY!

SLAM!

!!

WHAT THE *DEVIL?*

ALYCE IS UPSET WITH *MICHAEL?*

YES SIR.

MISS ALYCE...

...AND *MICHAEL* BEEN FIGHTIN' SOMETHIN' FIERCE!

WHA --?

WHAT?

51

MIKE?

AH'M SORRY AH GOT SO ANGRY,

AH MADE YOU A *MAKE-UP* PRESENT!

....
....

YOU'RE HORRI-BLE!

WHAT'S WRONG?!

ALYCE?

AH MADE MICHAEL TH' *LOVELIEST* PRESENT!

AND HE *HATES* IT!

....
....

OH?

MIKE?

NYEOWM!♥

YOU WANT TO *SNUGGLE UP* WITH ME?

IT'S OKAY. YOU COME RIGHT IN.

⸱GIGGLE!⸱ YOU'RE *DARLIN'*

AH *KNEW* YOU *LOVED* ME, MICHAEL.

FINE! *BE THAT WAY!*

AH *HATE* YOU!

ALYCE! WHAT *NOW?!*

AH THOUGHT MICHAEL WANTED TO *SLEEP WITH ME...*

...BUT HE WAS JUST COOOLD! WAAAA!

DEAR ...

LORD ...

AH!

YEWWWW

SIR! ARE YOU *ALL RIGHT?*

DON'T YOU GO *AILIN'* ON ME!

AH'M... AH'M *FINE...*

JUST A BIT... *PEAKED...*

THE COLONEL WAS REGRETTING THAT KITTENS GROW UP TO BE CATS...AND THAT SPOILED DAUGHTERS DON'T GROW UP AT ALL.

THE END

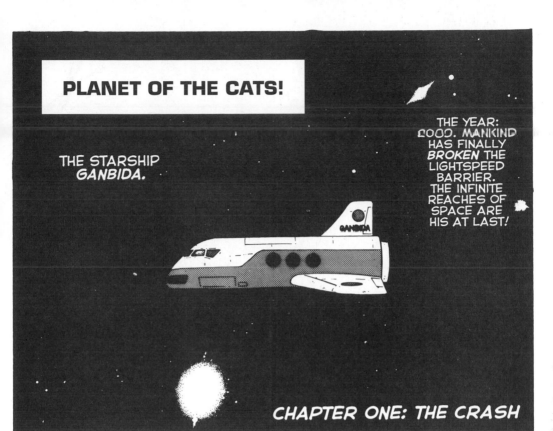

PLANET OF THE CATS!

THE STARSHIP *GANBIDA.*

THE YEAR: 2000. MANKIND HAS FINALLY *BROKEN* THE LIGHTSPEED BARRIER. THE INFINITE REACHES OF SPACE ARE HIS AT LAST!

CHAPTER ONE: THE CRASH

CAP-TAIN!

TIME FOR THE *TREADMILL!*

HANAKO, EXO-BIOLOGIST

I *ALREADY* TREAD-MILLED, DANGIT!

GIMME A *BREAK,* FOR PETE'S SAKE!

KONBAYASHI, CAPTAIN OF THE *GANBIDA.*

OH, NO YOU *DON'T,* CAPTAIN!

KAGEYAMA, ELECTRONICS SPECIALIST

58

WH-WHERE IS THIS PLACE?

AND... AM I...

...THE *ONLY* SURVIVOR?

AT... AT LEAST...

...I CAN BREATHE THE AIR.

I'VE GOT TO FIND THE OTHERS!!

AH?!

PUFF

IT'S...

IT'S A *CAT!*

A CAT IN A DRESS!!

WHICH MEANS THERE ARE *HUMANS* HERE!

FWWT

WAIT!

62

CHAPTER TWO: THE CAPTURE!

BUT THAT'S—! I'M *NOT*—

YAAAH!

KLONK

BACKSCRATCH UNIVERSITY BIOLOGICAL RESEARCH INSTITUTE

HRM. HMM, HNM.

THIS CREA-TURE IS—

--A SPECIES OF *ELE-PHANT SEAL!*

NOTHING TO FEAR. NOT POISONOUS.

ELE-PHANT SEAL! I *KNEW* IT!

I*!* AM*!* *NAWWWT!*

BY JOVE!

I'M A *HUMAN!* FROM A PLANET CALLED *EARTH!* MY NAME'S *HANAKO!*

OUR SPACESHIP WAS *DISABLED!* IT *CRASHED!*

PLEASE, LET ME *OUT!*

IT'S *TRUE!* IT *DOES* TALK!

PROFESSOR! I'M SCARED!

V-VERY WELL.

LET US *TEST* ITS IQ!

SEAL!

YOU WILL *ANSWER* MY QUESTIONS!

IF YOU DO NOT UNDERSTAND, *SAY SO!*

NOW, WHICH ONE...

...IS THE SAME AS THIS?!

THIS ONE.

BY JOVE!!

EEEK!

IT PASSED OUR UNIVERSITY ENTRANCE EXAM!

ITS IQ IS TERRIFYING!

TOLD YA!

WHAT'S THIS SEAL WORTH TO YOU?

IN-DEED.

FIFTEEN MEOWS! FINAL OFFER!

1 MEOW = APPROX. 130 YEN

FIF-TEEN?

C'MON, IT TALKS! UNSCREW YER WALLET, PROF.

BUT...OUR RESEARCH BUDGET--

I VEEL BUY FOR ZARTY MEOWS!

SHHNK

EH?

WHOA!

WHO ARE YOU?!

EPISODE THREE: THE PERFORMER

GREATEST SHOW ON FURTH!

THE HANAKO MONSTER!

ISN'T THIS EXCITING, MIKE? THAT ANIMAL WE CAUGHT, AT HER CIRCUS DEBUT!

HERE, I GOT YOU SARDINE CRACKERS AND CATNIP SODA.

THANKS, POPO.

MIKE... I'VE BEEN WONDERING. ARE WE *SURE* SHE'S AN ELEPHANT SEAL?

YEAH, I WAS KINDA WONDERING ABOUT THAT, TOO.

I BOUGHT AN ANIMAL GUIDE-BOOK TO CHECK.

BIG BOOK OF ANIMALS

THIS IS AN ELEPHANT SEAL

ELEPHANT SEAL
FAMILY: PHOCIDAE
CARNIVORE
WEIGHT: 2.5 TONS

I... AH... HMM.

THE NOSE...

BIG BOOK OF ANIMALS

W-WHY IT'S *JUST* LIKE HER!

YES. YES!

ELEPHANT SEAL! NO DOUBT!

LAD-EEEEZ AN' GENTLE-MAIN!

WELCOME TO ZE *GREATES'* SHOW ON FURTH-- KATZAWEENA'S *ZIRRRCUS!*

OHH, HERE IT *COMES!*

YOO ARE ABOUT TO ZEE--

--ZE MOS' *HIDEOUS* MONSTAR ON *FURTH,* BU' FARST...

...LET ME INTRAR-DUCE--

--BEAST MASTAIR DAIZUKE!

71

VAIT! SHE EES NOT ONLEE *FRAIGHTFUL!*

VATCH HANAKO *DANCE!* TO *MUSIC!*

NO!

IM-POSS-IBLE!

THAT THING?!

MUSIC, MAESTRO!

HY-AHH, HA-NAKO!

DANCE!

NO *DANCE*, NO *FISH!*

HEY!

WHSSKRAK

AH!

ALL *RIGHT*, AL-READY!

72

TP
TP
TP

KCHK

BEEP
BOOP
BOOP
BEEP
BOOP
BOOP

♫

HELLLO?

♪

HA-NA-KO!
HA-NA-KO!

CLAP
CLAP

CLAP

BRAVO!

CLAP

HA-
NA-
KO!

HA-NA-KO!
HA-NA-KO!

AM I GONNA DO THIS FOR... THE REST OF MY...LIFE?!

PART FOUR:
THE NEW BREED

ARE YOO KEEPINK ZE ZEAL *CLEAN?*

YES!

BUT THAT *HANAKO,* SHE HATES GETTIN' *SHAMPOOED.*

CLAWED ME PRETTY *BAD.*

I GAVE HER A *PIG* VACCINATION. DON' WANT HER TAKIN' *SICK.*

DO WHATAVAR YOU MUST. SHE EES ZE *ONLY WAN* IN ZE *WORLD.*

HEH HEH... ZO...

HAOW DO I PUMP ZHIS UP *EVEN MORE...?*

M-MISS KA-TARINA!

⸝HAHH⸜ BIG NEWS!

BAM!

HSSS!

VAT?

I'M *BUSY!*

BUT-- BUT *MA'AM!!*

ON THE ⸝HAFF⸜ *CATNIP COAST!*

THEY CAUGHT A *MALE!*

NUH--

NYEOWW?!

YER NOT THINKIN' OF *ESCAPIN'*, ARE YUH?

ESCAPE TO *WHERE*?!

MOMMA... PAPA... BIG SIS...

I-I'M... NEVER COMING HOME... ›SNIFF‹

AWWW...

....
....

SKTCH
SKTCI

PRR
RR
RRR

NYAMARU! EEMBECILE!

NO CURLING UP ON ZE ZEAL!

THMP

HOW ARE YOO, HANAKO DEAR?

KATZAWEENA'S BROUGHT YOO A PREZANT!

OH, RIGHT!!

LIKE THAT SHOT I GOT?

BETTAR! ZHIS!

GUHKK!

YERK

CAP--

CAPTAIN KONBAYASHI!

HANAKO! YEW MADE IT!

CAPTAIN! IT'S SO GOOD TO SEE YOU!

MYEH, HEH HEH. ZEALS OF A FLIPPER!

PURR-FECTO, BOSS!

THEY MATE, WE GET A PUP AND--

--WE OWN THE ELEPHANT SEAL MARKET!

YEZZZ.

GOOD MORNING, EVERYBODY! ♥

SUPER NEWS

IT'S TIME FOR... SUPER NEWS!

EPISODE FIVE: HOMESICK!

TODAY, OUR TOP STORY IS HANAKO!

REPORTER SUE IS ON LOCATION OUTSIDE OF KATARINA'S CIRCUS!

YOO-HOO, SUE!

HELLO, STUDIO!

TODAY WAS HANAKO'S ELEVENTH DATE, SUE! DID A CERTAIN SOMEONE GET LUCKY?

WELL...

...THEY DID HAVE A DATE...

81

FWSHHH

WHAT'S... THAT?

OUR SPACE SHUTTLE.

WE CRASHED HER HERE, BUT I FIXED HER!

FOR HANAKO!

HANAKO, BE STRONG! I'M COMING TO SAVE YOU!

I'M TAKING YOU HOME!

EPISODE SIX: THE GREAT ESCAPE

HOW ARE YOU GOING TO *RESCUE* HER?

SHE'S WATCHED BY *DEADLY GUARD CATS!*

HEH. I'VE GOT A *SECRET WEAPON.*

SECRET WEAPON?

THIS!

WHAT'S THAT *SPRAY?*

PSST

S-STINKS!

NYAOW!

THE SMELL! S-SO HORRIBLE!

MIKE, I'M DYING!

HEH HEH HEH... IT'S AN *ANTI-CAT EARTH WEAPON!* WORKS, HUH?

HSSST! YOU EARTH SEALS ARE MONSTERS!

VRRROOM

KATARINA CIRCUS

YOU STAY HERE.

I'LL GET HANAKO, AND YOU'LL TAKE US TO OUR SHUTTLE.

O-OKAY...

HUE 1994

HERE I GO!

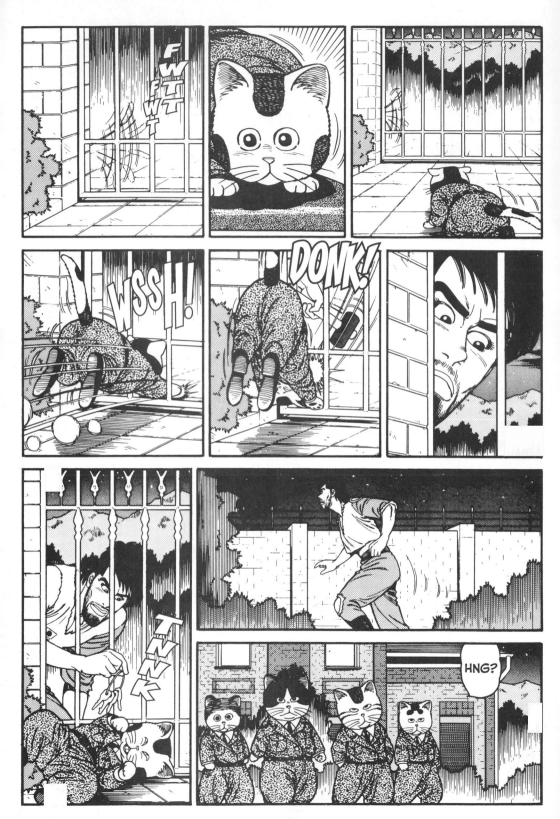

NYEOW!

AN ELEPHANT SEAL!

GET IT!

TMP TMP TMP

WE'LL GET A *RAISE* IF WE CATCH A *THIRD* ONE!

NO!

NUH--

YAWW! MY *NOSE!*

TMP TMP TMP TMP TMP

I QUIT! I *QUIT!* YAWWR!

NYAOWW!

THAT *SMELL!* IT'S *AWFUL!*

EEEEK!

STOP IT!

SHUT UP!

UHFF!

I SAID NO!

DANGIT, I WANT OUT!

WE GOTTA DO IT! SO WE'RE DOIN' IT NOW!

HELLLP!

HANA-KOOO!!

WHSSH

KAGEYAMA!

EPISODE SEVEN: FREEDOM!

93

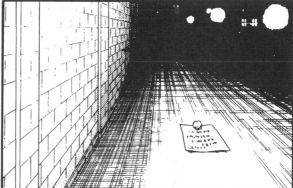

97

EPISODE EIGHT: ALL'S WELL THAT ENDS WELL

MICHAEL, POPO... WE OWE YOU *SO MUCH!*

HOW CAN WE EVER THANK--

NOW, D-DON'T...

⸢SNIFF!⸣ I-I'M CHOKING UP!

WAIT! MISS *HANAKO?*

YES?

ARE THERE *CATS* ON YOUR EARTH, TOO?

THERE SURE *ARE!* WE LIVE *TOGETHER!*

THEY CAN'T *TALK* LIKE YOU, THOUGH.

GOLLY! ♥

PLEASE SAY HI TO THE *EARTH CATS* FOR US!

I WILL! TAKE CARE, OKAY?

⋗SIGH⋖

YOU KNOW... ONLY *CATS* WOULD BELIEVE US!

I BET NO *HUMAN* WOULD.

THIS'LL BE LIKE OUR OWN LITTLE DREAM.

RROARRR

CHOOOOOM

HAHF! UHF!

AHFF! HFF! GHF!

WE JUST *HATE* TO ASK...

...BUT CAN YOU KEEP US UNTIL WE FIX OUR SHUTTLE AGAIN?

POPO, YOU JUST *RELAX!*

I'M MAKING DINNER!

PUT YOUR FEET *UP,* MICHAEL!

I'M *CATCHING FISH* FOR LATER!

UMM...

WELL...

CAN WE KEEP 'EM? THEY'RE NICE ENOUGH PETS.

THEY *ARE* HARD WORKERS... HOUSE-BROKEN, TOO.

AND SO IT WAS THAT *HANAKO* AND *KAGEYAMA* BECAME MICHAEL AND POPO'S *PETS!*

MEANWHILE, AT *KATARINA'S CIRCUS...*

CIRCUS

HEES *NEX'* TREEK--

--ZHEE *ELEPHAN' ZEAL* AN' ZHEE *PHONE!*

PLANET OF THE CATS--
THE END!
THANK YOU, KOBAYASHI-DONO!